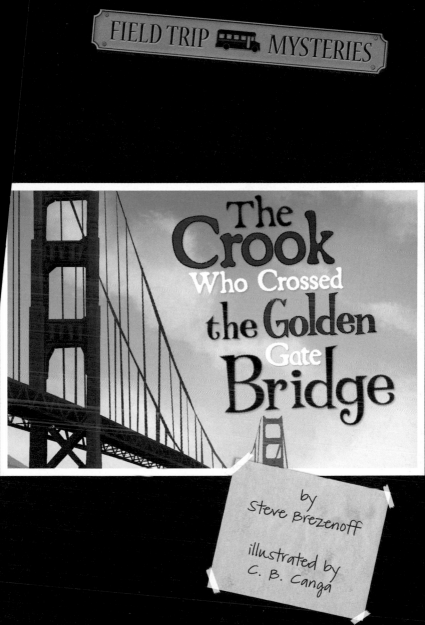

The Crook Who Crossed the Golden Gate Bridge

by
Steve Brezenoff

illustrated by
C. B. Canga

f Samantha Archer,

Field Trip Mysteries are published by Stone Arch Books
A Capstone Imprint
151 Good Counsel Drive, P.O. Box 669
Mankato, Minnesota 56002
www.capstonepub.com

Library of Congress Cataloging-in-Publication Data is
available on the Library of Congress website.

Library binding: 978-1-4342-2138-4
Paperback: 978-1-4342-2770-6

Art Director/Graphic Designer:
Kay Fraser

Summary:
In San Francisco on a field
trip, James "Gum" Shoo and his
friends get caught up in a wave
of pickpocketing.

Printed in the United States of America in Stevens Point,
Wisconsin.
042011

006170R

TABLE OF CONTENTS

James Shoo

A.K.A: (Gum)

D.O.B: November 19th

POSITION: 6th Grade

Is this because he chews a lot of gum?

INTERESTS:

Gum-chewing, field trips, and showing everyone what a crook Anton Gutman is.

KNOWN ASSOCIATES:

Archer, Samantha; Duran, Catalina; and Garrison, Edward.

NOTES:

Mr. Spade has made an effort to stc James from chewing gum in class. W fear he cannot be stopped.

CHAPTER ONE

CABLE CAR CROOK

I stared out of the bus window.

We were on the bus ride home.

The Golden Gate Bridge

and San Francisco were miles behind

us already, and most of the people on

the bus were asleep.

Samantha Archer, sitting in the aisle seat next to me, was snoring. I couldn't sleep, though. I should have been exhausted after that weekend, but I was still excited. Who wouldn't be!

I'd been looking forward to the sixth-grade trip to San Francisco for weeks. I always like field trips, but I had a special reason to be excited about this one. My mom's family used to live in San Francisco, way back before I was born, when my mom was a little girl. So I had been extra excited to see the place where she had lived.

It started when we drove into San Francisco over the Golden Gate Bridge on Friday morning. It was warm on the bus, but the air coming in through the open windows cooled us off as we crossed the bay.

"What a gorgeous day," my friend Cat said. She was sitting behind me and Sam, next to Edward — better known as Egg. (And I'm Gum. My real name is James, but my friends call me Gum.)

The bus pulled up to the hotel. Mr. Spade, our sixth-grade teacher, called for everyone to gather around. There were about twenty of us kids, plus some grownups who were chaperones.

"Okay, guys," Mr. Spade said. "We're going to leave our luggage here at the hotel, and then hop on the cable car for a quick tour of the city."

"Sounds like fun," Sam's grandmother said. Sam lives with her grandparents, and her grandmother decided to come along on this trip as one of the chaperones.

That was fine with me. Mrs. Archer is one of the coolest ladies I know.

The hotel's bellhops took our bags into the hotel on shiny golden carts. We followed Mr. Spade and Sam's grandmother as they led us toward the nearest place to catch a cable car. Mr. Spade handed out three-day passes to each of us. Those would let us ride the cable car system the whole weekend.

The cable car was crowded. Some of us got seats, but most of us had to stand, even hanging off the outside of the car!

I don't know how the conductor kept track of all the people jumping on and off, but he managed to check all our passes. There was one passenger I noticed that the conductor didn't see.

I elbowed Sam. "Check out that kid," I said. "He's been running away from the conductor for the last five minutes."

The guy looked younger than us, but not by too much. He was wearing a baseball cap low over his eyes.

Every time the conductor came anywhere near him, the kid would duck under some grownup's arms or legs and move to another part of the car.

"Looks like he's trying to get away without paying the fare," Sam said. She shook her head in disgust. "What a little crook."

Egg snapped a photo of him, but Cat just rolled her eyes. "He's probably just playing a game," she said. "He's not really a crook. Just a troublemaker."

Riding the cable car was a lot of fun, even with that little crook hanging around. We went up the biggest hill I'd ever seen and got to see a lot of the city.

By the time we got off the car, right back where we started, I was starving. "It's almost six," I said to Egg as we walked back toward the hotel. "Don't they have dinner in this city?"

Egg laughed and handed me a stick of gum. "Here," he said. "This'll take your mind off it."

I looked down at the stick and unwrapped the silver foil. "Mint?" I mumbled. "Boring!"

When we got into the lobby, Mr. Spade was standing at the front counter. He looked very upset.

"I can't believe this," he was saying to the man behind the desk. "My wallet has been stolen!"

Mr. Spade and the hotel manager spent an hour on the phone talking to a hundred different people.

My friends and I were lounging on one of the big couches in the lobby while Mr. Spade and the hotel manager sorted things out. "You guys," I said, "if I don't eat something soon, I might drop dead."

"Stop exaggerating," Cat said. "I'm sure we'll be eating dinner any minute."

Finally, Mr. Spade called everyone back over to the front desk. "Sorry for the delay, everyone," he said.

Mr. Spade put his hand on the shoulder of the man standing next to him. "This is Mr. Harley," he said. Mr. Harley was wearing a bright yellow shirt that said "Hotel Sunshine."

Mr. Spade went on, "Mr. Harley is the hotel manager. He's letting us check in after speaking to my credit card company. The pickpocket only got my credit card — which I've canceled, of course — twenty dollars, and my favorite photo of my cat, Cairo."

"Pickpocket?" Sam whispered to me, Egg, and Cat. "Gum, do you think it was . . ."

"That shady kid on the cable car," I finished for her. "Must have been!"

"Now, let's get some dinner!" Mr. Spade announced. "We're off to Chinatown."

Sam's grandmother led us to our bus.

"That kid looked like a crook to me," Egg said. Sam nodded slowly, and we all climbed onto the bus.

"I haven't been to San Francisco's Chinatown in probably fifty years," Sam's grandmother said. She sat in front of Sam and me, and across the aisle from Egg and Cat, right in the front of the bus. "Maybe sixty years."

"Oh come on, Grandma," Sam said. "You're only sixty-two."

"Hush," Sam's grandmother said. "Don't interrupt. Back then, San Francisco was a magical place. Lots of famous crime movies were set here."

"That's true," Sam said. "Some of my favorite movies, like *The Maltese Falcon*."

Sam's grandmother nodded. "That's right," she said. "This weekend, we'll be walking the same streets walked by Sam Spade."

Sam smiled. "I was named after him," she said proudly.

"San Francisco is important in my family, too," I said. "My mom and her parents lived in Chinatown when she was a little girl."

"Really?" Cat asked. "I thought your family always lived in River City."

I shook my head. The bus's brakes squeaked and we came to a stop. I looked out the window and saw the famous dragon gate.

"Nope," I said. "My mom's family moved to River City after she finished elementary school. She loves to talk about Chinatown, but I've never been here before."

We all climbed off the bus to pick a place to have dinner. I couldn't wait. The smells coming out of all the restaurants were so good! Finally we all agreed on a noodle shop.

It was amazing. We all had different kinds of soup. Cat used chopsticks to eat her vegetarian noodle soup. I used a spoon for my chicken soup, but the noodles kept slipping off of it. Sam slurped up her noodles in beef broth. And Egg? Well, he had egg drop soup.

As we all walked slowly back to the bus, a cable car came rambling by.

"Mr. Spade!" Sam cried out. "Let's ride the cable car back to the hotel."

Mr. Spade smiled and waved his hands. "Not me, Samantha," he said. "I don't need my pockets picked again, thank you. But if your grandmother wants to take you, anyone who wants to certainly may."

Sam's grandma said, "That's fine with me!" A handful of us jumped on the car. This time the car was even more crowded. No one got a seat, not even Mrs. Archer.

"I think this might be our best field trip yet," I said as we jumped off the cable car near the hotel. "Family history, crime movies, delicious noodles . . . what more can you ask for?"

Cat laughed. "It has been fun so far," she said. "Too bad about Mr. Spade's wallet, though."

Sam's grandmother nodded. "That was a real shame," she said. "That's why I always keep my wallet inside my zipped-up pocket book."

"Um, Grandma?" Sam said. She grabbed her grandmother's bag. "Look!"

We all stopped and looked. The zipper on the bag was wide open!

"Oh no!" Sam's grandmother said. She dug through the bag for a few minutes. "My wallet is gone!"

The five of us sat down on the big lobby couch. Sam's grandmother was very upset.

"Did you have all your credit cards in your purse?" Sam asked.

Her grandmother nodded. "Of course," she said. "And all our traveler's checks, too."

"I'll call the credit card company," Sam said, "and the bank. We'll get it all straightened out."

Sam and her grandma walked away to a pay phone in the lobby. Egg, Cat, and I just sat there, sometimes shaking our heads, or mumbling, "This stinks."

Suddenly, I spotted someone skulking around near the potted palm trees by the front desk.

"Egg, Cat," I said. "Look at that." I pointed at the kid.

"That boy?" Cat said. "What about him?"

"Does he look familiar to you?" I asked.

Egg clicked through the pictures on his camera until he came to one of the boy from the cable car.

"Yup," he said. "That's the pickpocket, all right."

Across the lobby, Sam looked up. She saw the kid too and dropped the phone. "Hey! That's him!" she yelled.

An instant later, she was sprinting across the lobby toward the little crook. When I got a good look at his face, I was even more sure it was the same boy we'd spotted on the cable car.

"Get him!" Sam shouted. She ran toward the boy, and Egg, Cat, and I followed her.

The boy saw us coming. He started to run. We should have known he'd be quick. He'd have to be fast to keep away from that conductor on the cable car, after all.

Soon, the kid ducked through a door next to the elevator.

"He went into the stairwell!" Sam shouted. "Come on!"

Sam was tall and really fast, way faster than Cat and Egg and me. We struggled to keep up as she charged up the stairs ahead of us.

When we were almost to the third floor, I heard a door slam.

"This way," I said to Cat and Egg when we reached the door. I pulled the heavy door open just in time to see Sam race around the far corner.

"Can't we stop for a minute? And catch our breath?" Cat said.

"And let Sam face that crook alone?" I asked. "No way."

Egg, Cat, and I huffed and puffed our way around the corner. The door at the far end of the hall slammed closed. It led to the other stairwell.

Sam called to us, "He went back downstairs! Hurry up."

Going down the steps was a lot easier than going up. We soon ran right back into the lobby, and spotted the boy running at top speed across the hotel. Sam was close behind him. Suddenly, the hotel manager stepped out of his office.

"Mr. Harley!" Sam called out. "Stop that boy. He's a pickpocket!"

The manager just looked at Sam, confused. As we watched, the boy ran right up to Mr. Harley and threw his arms around the manager's waist.

"Huh?" Sam said. Her sneakers squeaked on the marble floor as she came to a stop. "Do you know this boy?" she asked Mr. Harley. "He's a pickpocket!"

"This isn't a pickpocket," Mr. Harley said. "This is Jake Harley. My son."

CHAPTER FOUR

DENIALS

"The pickpocket is your son?" I asked.

"I wish you'd stop saying that," Mr. Harley said. "My son is not a pickpocket."

"We're sorry to have to be the ones to tell you, Mr. Harley," Sam said. She glared at Jake. "But we saw him on the cable car this afternoon. And then Mr. Spade's wallet was gone. And now my grandmother's wallet was stolen, and he showed up in the hotel at the same time we did!"

I nodded. "Also, on the cable car, he was pushing everyone, and knocking people around," I said. "Plus, he didn't pay the fare. He hid from the conductor."

Jake looked at his feet. Mr. Harley turned his son around to face him. "Are these children telling the truth?" Mr. Harley asked.

Jake didn't say anything for a few moments.

"Come on, Jake," Mr. Harley said. "Answer me."

Jake sniffed. "It's not true," he said. "I didn't pick anything from anyone's pockets."

"And what about the other part?" Mr. Harley said. "The part about not paying the fare."

Jake nodded. "That part is true," he admitted.

Sam gritted her teeth. "He's lying," she said. "I know crooks, and your son is a crook!"

"I am not a crook!" Jake said. "Besides, I didn't just get back to the hotel. I was having dinner in the kitchen with Millie. I've been in the kitchen since Jack and I got off the cable car this afternoon."

Mr. Harley sighed. "He does always have dinner in the kitchen," he said. "And he usually spends hours there, just chatting with Jack and the kitchen crew."

Jake turned to the four of us. "Listen, I'm sorry for bumping into someone, if I did, which I didn't mean to," he said. "But I swear, I didn't take anyone's wallet. Honest."

"I'll deal with my son's behavior on the cable car," Mr. Harley said. "Thank you for letting me know."

Jake kicked at the marble floor and a loud squeak filled the lobby.

My friends and I looked at each other. Without a word, we stepped away. It was time to leave them alone to deal with Jake's criminal behavior.

Just then, Mr. Spade and the others who had taken the bus back arrived. They filled the lobby. Mrs. Archer told Mr. Spade about her wallet disappearing. "That's too bad," Mr. Spade said, patting her hand. "We'll make sure you and Sam have enough spending money while you're here."

"Luckily, Sam took care of the credit cards," Mrs. Archer said. "And I'll call the police from my room to file a report."

"Good thinking," Mr. Spade said. He noticed us all watching and added, "All right, everyone. Let's get cleaned up and rested. Tomorrow is going to be a big day."

"What are we doing tomorrow?" I asked, dreaming about that noodle shop.

Mr. Spade smiled. "Tomorrow morning we're off to Alcatraz!" he said.

"The prison?"

A huge smile formed on Sam's face.

"This is going to be so cool."

CHAPTER FIVE

TO PRISON!

I'm pretty sure the tour of Alcatraz was one of Sam's most exciting days ever. The whole time we were in the prison, she just kept smiling and whispering, "This is so awesome."

We'd taken a cable car and a boat ride to get to the prison island. The tour guide showed us a prisoner cell, and told us about the famous escape. Everyone used to say no one could escape from Alcatraz, but three prisoners had escaped one night.

"What a great story," Sam said.

"That's why they made a movie about it," her grandmother said. Sam nodded.

After our tour of the jail, we watched a short video about the island. Even Sam hadn't known it used to be a fort, during the Civil War!

The guide led us all over the island outside the prison, too. We went through gardens and saw some cool birds. We learned that Alcatraz was completely empty before people started planting things over 150 years ago.

After the tour, we headed back to the boat to return to the mainland. Sam, Mrs. Archer, Egg, Cat, and I stood at the boat's railing as we sailed away from Alcatraz Island.

"Oh, this ocean air sure makes me sleepy," Sam's grandmother said after the ferry had pulled away from the dock. "I'm going to take a seat on a bench inside."

"Okay, Grandma," Sam said. "I'll come wake you up when we dock."

Sam's grandmother walked off, and the four of us leaned on the railing. The wind was loud, but we didn't mind. It was pretty cool to feel the spray on our faces.

"So," Sam said, "what do you guys think about Jake Harley?"

Cat shrugged. "I believe him," she said. "He told the truth about not paying the fare. I think he's an honest kid — mostly."

"Once a thief, always a thief," Sam said. She shook her head and added, "A tiger can't change its stripes."

"I'm with Sam,"
I said.
"He's a crook."

"Sorry, Cat," Egg said. "I think he's lying too. Sure, he admitted that he'd skipped out on the fare. But who knows if he only admitted that so it would seem like he was telling the truth about not being the pickpocket."

Cat sighed, but we outvoted her. Jake Harley was our number-one suspect.

"We should check in with Millie in the kitchen," Sam said. "She can confirm Jake's story."

The cable car back from the dock to the hotel wasn't very crowded. There were plenty of empty seats, so Sam's grandmother grabbed one right away.

"Hey, look at that girl's shirt," Sam said. She's always the first one to spot important clues.

Next to Sam's grandmother was a girl. She was older than us, probably sixteen or seventeen. She was wearing a bright yellow shirt, just like Mr. Harley's. On the chest it said "Hotel Sunshine." On her lap, the girl had a box overflowing with fresh lettuce.

Cat smiled at her. "Hi," she said. "Do you work at the Hotel Sunshine?"

The girl slowly looked up at Cat. "What do you think?" she asked. She shook her head and sighed.

Cat glanced at me and I shrugged. "You work in the kitchen, right?" Cat asked.

The girl looked at the box of lettuce in her lap. "No, I fix the air conditioners," she said, rolling her eyes. "Of course I work in the kitchen."

The girl looked out the window, so we figured she was done talking to us.

"She's pretty rude," Egg said quietly.

Cat smiled. "I guess some people just don't like to chat," she said.

"Well," Sam said, "she works in the kitchen, and we have to talk to Millie anyway. How do you guys feel about tailing her?"

EMPLOYEES ONLY

"Everyone get cleaned up for lunch,"
Mr. Spade announced when we got back to
the hotel. The rest of the class headed up to
their rooms, but Sam, Cat, Egg, and I hung
back. We kept an eye on the girl from the
cable car. When no one was looking, we
carefully snuck after her.

She walked slowly, so it was easy to
keep up. But soon she pushed open a big
swinging door. A sign on the door read,
"Employees Only!"

"Should we follow her?" Cat said. She was obviously worried.

Sam nodded. "We have to," she said. "It's for justice. Besides, we have to find Millie, and I think this door goes to the kitchen."

I took a deep breath and looked at Egg, then Cat. We nodded, so Sam pushed open the door.

We peered down a long hallway. The walls were all metal, and the floor was speckled gray tile.

From the far end of the hall we could hear banging and clanking of pots and pans. The girl from the cable car was nowhere to be seen.

"I guess we lost her," Cat said. She stayed behind me and Egg.

"Maybe we should just head upstairs to get ready for lunch," I said.

"We can't give up now," Sam said. "Let's just find Millie."

She started to walk down the hall toward the sounds. The rest of us followed her.

We passed a pair of swinging doors. I peeked through the window and saw a huge room, filled with tables and chairs. No one seemed to be inside.

Cat came up next to me. "I think that room is probably the Sunset Room," she said. "That's the hotel restaurant, where we're having lunch."

We caught up to Sam and Egg. They had stopped at the end of the hall, and Sam was carefully trying to peek around the corner.

"It's the kitchen," she said. "I can see the girl from the cable car. She's putting the vegetables away in the giant walk-in refrigerator."

"Now what?" Egg said. "Do we just stand here until someone catches us?"

Sam took a deep breath. "Let's confront her," she said.

"Her?" Cat said. "Why? She didn't do anything, besides act rudely."

Sam narrowed her eyes. "True," she said.

And then we all jumped about ten feet in the air, because from behind us someone said, "Hey! What are you kids doing back here?!"

DEAD END

"Are you from the school group?" the woman asked. She was old. Older than Sam's grandmother. She was wearing a bright yellow top. But this shirt was different from Mr. Harley's and the girl on the cable car. It was a chef's shirt, and on one side it said "Millie" in fancy letters.

"Um, yes," Cat said. "We're —"

Sam stepped in front of Cat and said, "Lost! We're lost. We were looking for Jake, Mr. Harley's son. We're friends of his."

Cat whispered, "Sam! Don't tell her that."

Sam shushed her and smiled at Millie.

"You're friends of Jake's?" Millie asked. She frowned and looked at us carefully. "He never mentioned you."

"Oh, um, we just met," I said, trying to cover quickly. "Have you seen him?"

"Not since dinner last night," Millie said. "He always has dinner with me and Jack. Last night was just me and Jake, though. Jack was busy all morning and evening running errands for me."

"Oh, I see," Sam said.

Millie looked around. "You know, I sent Jack on another errand this morning, hours ago," she said. "It shouldn't take this long."

"Oh, um, well, thanks," Sam said. "I guess we better get going."

Millie was too distracted looking for Jack, and we hurried away, back down the long metal hallway.

"This Jack person sounds important," Sam said as we reached the lobby. "He wasn't at dinner with Millie and Jake last night, after all. No alibi."

"Well, but whoever he is, he was running an errand for Millie," Egg pointed out. "So, that's an alibi, right? That proves he wasn't the person who stole the wallet."

Sam smirked. "I suppose so," she said. "But he's obviously someone who works in the kitchen. Let's keep an eye on this kitchen staff."

"Speaking of kitchens, lunch now?" Cat asked. "I've had enough sneaking around and telling lies for today."

Sam chuckled. "Okay," she said, "but you'll never make a great private eye with that attitude."

Cat waved her off. "Fine with me," she said. "I'm just relieved Jake wasn't lying. He really didn't steal your grandmother's wallet."

"I guess not,"
Sam said.

"Which means we are
out of suspects."

CRIME WAVE

Lunch was nothing special. Grilled cheese and French fries. Typical stuff. The only interesting thing about it was the girl from the cable car. She was our table's waiter! Boy, the face she made when she saw the four of us sitting there, smiling at her. She was pretty annoyed to see us.

After lunch, we all took the bus to the San Francisco Museum of Modern Art.

"Boring," I muttered to my friends as the bus pulled up.

"No way," Cat said. She was on the edge of her seat. Even Egg was excited.

Sam and I just shook our heads. "Walking around some stuffy museum is not my idea of a good time," Sam said. "We should be trying to solve this crime wave."

"Crime wave?" Cat said. "You're crazy. I bet Mr. Spade's pickpocket and your grandmother's pickpocket have nothing to do with each other. I say we forget about it."

"I'm with Cat," Egg said. "Let's just enjoy the rest of our trip."

The museum wasn't as boring as I thought it would be. Some of the sculptures were pretty cool, actually. They looked like giant metal spiders.

Sam found a painting by Andy Warhol called "Red Liz." Sam said she was a big actress about a hundred years ago, I guess, named Elizabeth Taylor.

"She was the most famous woman in the world, back then," Sam explained. Her grandmother stood behind her, nodding and smiling. She looked proud of Sam.

Even though the museum wasn't that bad, I was still glad when it was time to go. I was hoping we'd go back to that noodle shop for dinner. We got back onto the cable car. The annoyed waitress was on the car again, and she pretended not to see us.

As we got off the cable car, I was almost knocked over by a crazy woman running down the sidewalk.

"Officer!" she was shouting. "Help, help! Police!"

A uniformed cop was standing near the hotel. He jogged over to the woman.

She was totally out of breath, and a few of us from the sixth-grade class gathered around her and the cop while she tried to talk. "Officer," the woman managed to say, "I've been robbed!"

"Try to stay calm, ma'am," the cop said. He was a young guy, and he seemed nervous. I could tell he was trying his hardest to stay cool. "When did this happen?"

The woman shook her head. "I don't know," she said. "I just reached into my purse to pay my cable car fare, and my wallet was gone."

The cop nodded. "The cable car," he said. "I figured. We've had a run of pickpockets reported on the cable cars in the last forty-eight hours."

Sam elbowed Cat. "Ow!" Cat snapped. Sam dragged the three of us away from the cop and the woman.

"What did I tell you?" Sam whispered. "It's a crime wave, just like I said."

"Fine," Cat said. "You were right. But still, what are we supposed to do? We're out of suspects, remember?"

Sam narrowed her eyes and bit a fingernail. "I'm not giving up," she said. "We're close. The hotel is involved. I can feel it."

A SISTER

When we got back to the hotel, Mr. Harley was behind the front desk. Jake was next to him. Jake looked pretty upset.

"What's going on?" Sam asked. She started to walk right over to the two of them.

"Sam!" Cat hissed after her. "Stop! Stay out of it!"

But it was too late. As soon as Jake spotted Sam walking over, he ran through a door, slamming it behind him.

"Jake, come back!" Mr. Harley called after him, but Jake ignored him.

"Why did that boy take off like that?" Sam's grandmother asked us. We just shrugged.

Mr. Harley sighed. "He didn't want you kids to see him so upset," he said quietly. "You see, he's just been so sad since his mother got ill. He's really worried about her."

"Oh no," Sam's grandmother said. "I hope it's nothing too serious."

Mr. Harley smiled at her. "She'll be okay," he said. "But it's hard for the kids. And for now, she can't work. Money has been tight. You know how it is."

Sam's grandmother nodded and patted his hand.

"Jack's been working long hours,"
Mr. Harley said. "But it never seems like
enough. I guess that's why Jake thought
it would be a good idea to skip out on the
fare."

I felt awful. It's one thing to try to catch
a pickpocket, but we didn't know Jake's
mother was so sick. Of course he'd been
acting weird. I'd act weird too.

Then Sam frowned. "Wait a minute,"
she said. "Who's Jack? The same Jack that
eats lunch with Millie and Jake?"

Mr. Harley nodded. "Of course," he said.
"Jack is Jake's older sister."

"Jack is a girl?" I asked.

My friends and I glanced at each other.

"Yes," Mr. Harley said.

"It's short for Jacklyn. She works in the kitchen with Millie. She was your waitress today at lunch."

* * *

At dinner that evening, Sam put her salad fork down and leaned forward. She always does that when she's about to say something really important.

"Guys," she said, "I know what's going on."

"You do?" I said. "I'm still confused about a girl being named Jack!"

Egg and Cat laughed, but Sam just shook her head. "This is serious," she said. "We have to catch the pickpocket, and I have a plan to do it."

So she told us her plan. It sounded crazy to us, but Sam was sure it would work. After dinner, we said good night, but I knew with Sam's plans waiting for us in the morning, sleep wouldn't come easily.

THE BIG PLAN

"This is it," Sam said over breakfast the next morning. "Time to act out my big plan."

The four of us sat around a table in the Sunset Room watching our waiter, Jack the girl, wipe down the buffet counter.

"If my guess is right," Sam went on, "as soon as Jack is done clearing the tables, she'll run out on some errand. Then we tail her."

"Got it," I said.

Cat shook her head. "I don't like this plan, Sam," she said. "I feel like we should stay out of it."

"After how rude she was to you on the cable car?" Sam asked.

Cat shrugged. "I don't mind," she said. "Especially now that I know she is so upset about her mom's illness."

"We all agreed to the plan, Cat," I said. "We can't back out now."

Cat sighed. "Fine," she said. "But if things get weird, we come back to the hotel, okay?"

"And we get the cops," Sam added. "Promise."

After all the tables were cleared, Jack went through the swinging double doors.

"Okay, everyone," Mr. Spade called from the main doors of the Sunset Room. "Let's get moving. Lots to do today."

"That includes you four," Sam's grandmother said. She was standing at our table, waiting for us to get up, but we couldn't take our eyes off the swinging doors. Why didn't Jack come back in?

"Um, just a second, Grandma," Sam said. "Uh, Egg isn't feeling so good. He probably had a bad piece of sausage or something."

"What?" Egg said. "Oh, um, right. Sausage. Ow. My tummy."

"Well, should I find the hotel doctor?" Sam's grandmother said.

"Oh no!" Egg said, jumping to his feet. "I'll be fine in a minute."

"Right, we just need to sit for a minute," Sam said. Just then, Jack came through the swinging doors. She was holding an empty produce crate. "Okay, now we can go," Sam added.

Sam's grandmother stared at us like we were crazy as we jumped up from the table and followed Jack out of the Sunset Room. She went right through the lobby and through the big revolving door of the hotel. Sam was hot on her tail, so we did the best we could to keep up.

"Hey, where are you kids going?" Sam's grandmother called after us. "Stop!"

"Sorry, Grandma," Sam said over her shoulder. "We're on a case."

"What are you talking about?" her grandmother asked.

But Mrs. Archer could barely keep up with me, Egg, and Cat. Her speedy granddaughter was way ahead of all of us.

"We're about to solve the pickpocket crimes," Egg explained as we hurried after Sam. A cable car pulled up and Jack climbed on. Sam followed her. "We have to hurry!" Egg added.

"Solving a crime?" Sam's grandmother repeated with a twinkle in her eye. She was obviously a lot like her granddaughter. "Well . . . I suppose as long you have a chaperone with you, it'll be fine."

She smiled, and we all climbed aboard the cable car.

We found Sam on the crowded car. She was sneaking glances at Jack, who was standing among the crowd at the front of the car.

"Is that the mark?" her grandmother asked quietly.

Sam nodded. "She's the punk who ripped off your roll," she said out of the side of her mouth. "I've got my peepers on her, though. One false move and it's curtains."

Don't ask me what any of that meant. Sam and her grandmother speak a different language half the time.

Just then, the conductor came over. We all pulled out our passes.

"Sir," Sam said, "do you see that girl over there, in the bright yellow shirt?"

The conductor looked over his shoulder, then back at Sam. "Yeah, so?" he said.

"Well, that's the cable car pickpocket," Sam said. "The one responsible for the crime wave."

"Is that right?" the conductor said.

"Sam!" Cat snapped. "We don't know for sure."

"It all fits, though," Sam said quietly. "She's desperate for money, and she's always been on an errand, riding the cable cars, when the crimes took place."

The conductor squinted at her. "That isn't much proof," he said. He seemed to be thinking it over. "I'll tell you what. I still haven't collected fares from the front. I'll keep an eye on her. Fair enough?"

"Thank you," Sam's grandmother said. "I'm afraid my granddaughter enjoys fighting crime a little too much sometimes."

"It's an admirable trait," the conductor said. He headed toward the front of the car.

Jack had been watching us. When she saw the conductor heading toward her, she pushed through the crowd. The car slowed down a little, and she jumped off.

"Stop!" the conductor cried.

At once, the car screeched to a halt and the conductor jumped off in hot pursuit. We didn't want to miss the action, so we all jumped off too.

Jack's yellow shirt was impossible to miss, even in the crowded San Francisco rush hour streets. The conductor caught her in no time.

"Get off me!" Jack screamed as the conductor grabbed her shirt. As she tried to get away, a head of lettuce flew out of the crate she was carrying.

"Why are you running?" Sam asked.

"I'm not running," Jack said quickly. "I just missed my stop."

The conductor waved over a police officer who was across the street. "I think maybe you should take a look through this young woman's crate," the conductor said when the cop walked up.

"Is that right?" the cop said. "Looks to me like it's full of lettuce."

Sam and her grandma laughed.

"She must have filled it with lettuce before she even left the kitchen," I said, "so she would have someplace to hide the wallets she stole!"

The cop pushed aside the greenery and revealed three wallets at the bottom of the crate. "Well, well," the cop said to the conductor. "It looks you've caught the cable car pickpocket."

"Don't give me the credit," the conductor said. "It was these four kids."

We smiled at the cop. "Great job," he said. "A few commuters will be very thankful to have their wallets back."

The cop put Jack in handcuffs and walked her to his police car.

"Oh my gosh," I said, as I looked at the head of lettuce rolling down the street.

"What?" Cat asked.

"I just remembered
the salad we had
at dinner last night,"
I told her.
"We were eating
the evidence!"

Back at the hotel, Sam's grandmother led us over to Mr. Harley. Millie and Jake were with him. The rest of the sixth grade was gathered in the lobby. They'd all been wondering where we were.

Mr. Spade joined us to talk to the hotel manager, and Sam's grandmother explained to him about the pickpocket case.

"We're awfully sorry about Jack," Sam said to Mr. Harley.

Mr. Harley nodded. "I knew she was upset and worried about money," he said, shaking his head sadly, "but I had no idea she'd do anything this crazy."

Cat patted his hand. "I'm sure the judge will be understanding," she said. "Once he hears the whole story."

Mr. Harley sighed. "She's only sixteen," he said. "I hope you're right. But still, Jack will have to take her punishment."

Mr. Spade and Sam's grandmother continued talking to Mr. Harley as my friends and I walked off. Egg, Cat, and I turned to Sam.

"So," I said, "why were you and your grandmother laughing about the lettuce?"

"Yeah," Cat said. "It didn't seem that funny."

Sam smiled. "Don't you get it? We should have known the whole time," she said. "Lettuce is old-movie slang for cash!"

I rolled my eyes. But I knew for the rest of my life, whenever I ate noodles or salad, I'd think of the crime wave we squashed in San Francisco.

literary news

MYSTERIOUS WRITER REVEALED!

Steve Brezenoff lives in St. Paul, Minnesota, with his wife, Beth, their son, Sam, and their small, smelly dog, Harry. Besides writing books, he enjoys playing video games, riding his bicycle, and helping middle-school students work on their writing skills. Steve's ideas almost always come to him in his dreams, so he does his best writing in his pajamas.

arts & entertainment

CALIFORNIA ARTIST IS KEY TO SOLVING MYSTERY – POLICE SAY

Early on, C. B. Canga's parents discovered that a piece of paper and some crayons worked wonders in taming the restless dragon. There was no turning back. In 2002 he received his BFA in Illustration from the Academy of Arts University in San Francisco. He works at the Academy of Arts as a drawing instructor. He lives in California with his wife, Robyn, and his three kids.

A Detective's Dictionary

alibi (AL-i-bye)–a claim that a person accused of a crime was somewhere else when the crime was committed

chaperone (SHAP-ur-ohn)–someone who watches over others

conductor (kuhn-DUHK-tur)–someone who collects fares

confront (kun-FRUNT)–talk to someone face to face

denials (di-NYE-uhlz) statements that something did not happen

exaggerating (eg-ZAJ-uh-rate-ing)–making something seem bigger, better, or more important than it really is

honest (ON-ist)–someone who is truthful and will not lie, steal, or cheat

pickpocket (PIK-pok-it)–someone who steals from people's pockets or handbags

pursuit (pur-SOOT)–trying to catch someone

responsible (ri-SPON-suh-buhl)–caused something to happen

skulking (SKUHLK-ing)–sneaking around

suspect (SUHSS-pekt)–someone thought to be responsible for a crime

(A)

San Francisco

When we visited San Francisco on our sixth grade field trip, I didn't expect to be solving a mystery! The thing I was most excited about was visiting Chinatown, where my mom's family lived when she was a little girl.

San Francisco's Chinatown is the oldest Chinatown in North America and the biggest one outside of Asia. In addition, it has the largest Chinese population in the United States.

The first Chinese immigrants arrived in San Francisco in 1848. Now, more than 100,000 people live in the area, which co only a little more than 1 square mile.

Chinatown is known for its big, elaborate Chinese-style buildings, shaped like pagodas. It is also famous for its food. There are more than 300 restaurants in Chinatown, serving traditional Chinese food like mooncakes, dim sum, and hot tea.

Chinatown is a big tourist attraction, but it is also a living neighborhood. Still, it gets more visitors every year than the Golden Gate Bridge.

Very good, James! It must have been interesting to visit the place where your family once lived. I'm still dreaming about that noodle soup . . .   -Mr. S.

FURTHER INVESTIGATIONS

CASE #FTMO6GSF

1. Jake and Jack are worried about their sick mom. What are some good things to do when you're worried?

2. What was the coolest thing the kids saw on this field trip? If you were in San Francisco, what would you want to visit?

3. In a small group, talk about a mystery that's happened at your school. Come up with a list of suspects. Can you solve the mystery?

IN YOUR OWN DETECTIVE'S NOTEBOOK...

1. Pretend you're Jake. Write a letter to me (Gum), telling me what's been going on since the field trip.

2. I was interested in visiting San Francisco because my family has roots there. Where is your family from? Write about it.

3. If you could go anywhere on a field trip, where would you go? Write about your dream field trip.